I0620830

Volume I

THE PINK PARCHMENT POEMS

Poems written on the pages of my soul

Kenyetta Freeman

TABLE OF CONTENTS

WATER OF LIFE

I guess if He finishes all of my sentences, then I could

at least stop,

take a look and listen.

When that Light hit us, believers

we more than glow, we glisten.

Anointed for this work,

He signed sealed and delivered her.

To Him, she's the apple of His eye.

He ain't ashamed of her and she ain't ashamed of

Him.

Waited patiently I did that,

now I'm trying to drink from the river where there is no

lack and sit underneath the trees with leaves that

are healing for the nations.

So, when He called I answered.

And now, I've got myself a revelation.

HOLY GHOST

Holy Ghost gangster, I've been that,

still, no two snowflakes are alike.

Sometimes I wonder, why are things so shifty?

Nothing's ever stable.

Regardless of the situation, I've got to be able to stand.

Bible in one hand, the Oil of Anointing in the other.

Please, Holy Ghost comfort me.

There is no other, that can teach me like You,

speak to me like You do.

Pray for me how You do.

Let me walk in You.

Yes, it's true. You grace me for battle and strengthened
me for the fight

and when it's time to go toe to toe with my foe, You unleash the Spirit of might.

Jesus baptized me in You.

I love the way that You lead me.

Lack is no match for the way that You sustain me.

Your presence is so much more than an essence,

still, I need more of You.

Burn everything up in me that doesn't look like You.

You're the only restraining power in the world.

Please don't ever leave me.

So, while you're passing by

Please, remember me.

BACKDROP

I guess if He's changing the backdrop, then He's changing the scenery, the circumstances, the climate, the atmosphere, the ambiance, the picture, everything.

Some things are going to be beautiful.

Whatever is environmentally unsuitable for me, in this time is His for the taking.

And no I haven't arrived, I'm still in the making.

Until the day that Christ returns, I'm constantly being perfected.

All that praying in tongues, I've erected.

An edifice within me that is kind of like a fortress.

Fortified by His strength, no weapon formed against me shall prosper.

Sickness has to move out of the way,

Jehovah Rapha, He is my Doctor.

He heals terminal illnesses by way of a miracle.

He's the same yesterday, today and forever,

no, He's not fickle.

He doesn't lie.

The prophetic words spoken over my life shall come to pass

and I'm not worried about my past anymore

because it's in the past.

And the test that you just came out of

I hear Him saying that "you passed"

and don't worry about the fact that they overlooked you, the last shall be first and the first shall be last.

He's moving us into new realms and new dimensions, I'm talking new levels. Go deeper.

In this season, He's amplifying new voices and He will be their speaker.

To the preacher that has been preaching Jesus to an empty crowd,

get ready,

because you're going to need a reader.

DIVINE RELEASE

May you have an abundance of God's grace that allows you to have the clarity, extreme focus and precision that is required to effectively execute the plan of God for your life.

May you have godly wisdom, knowledge and understanding to discern divine destiny encounters and heavenly hookups.

May you super-abound in the peace of God, knowing that your commanded blessing has already been released and that every prophetic word spoken over your life shall come to pass.

May the Spirit of Might come upon you that will cause you to prevail practically, in prayer and in spiritual warfare.

May the weapons of your warfare be fortified with Holy Ghost fire!

May you have an anointing that allows you to persevere and outperform every agent of Satan and every enemy that has been sent to cause havoc in your life.

And may you push past your pain and plow onward toward your future.

Because your future is blessed, bright, beautiful and has already been ordained by God before the foundation of the world.

So, dance. Dance in the glory of God.

DEUTROS

Knowing this that with Christ nothing shall be impossible.

Why do things seem so far beyond my reach?

I'm trying to press towards the mark of the prize of the high calling.

I know that God is able.

To bring the prophetic words spoken over my life to pass.

God is able.

To heal me from the wounds of my past.

God is able.

To cause me to be first because I was always last.

Yes. My God is able.

Mighty, perfect, just. Awesome in all His ways.

When I look back over my life oftentimes, I'm amazed.

Look, He kept me from the dangers lurking around the corner.

Even when I was literally sleeping with the enemy.

God protected me. Rescued me, saved me from myself.

My past is colorful, so you got to excuse me when I speak about Him. I get excited.

Death was looking me dead in my eyes. What would I do without Him?

After the accident, the truck was so messed up.

How can I live without Him?

They could have locked me up for 25-99.

I can't go without Him.

Freed from promiscuity. I can breathe without Him.

So, when I smell a lion in waiting, I'm not waiting. Self-preservation, my God covers me.

Careful to not become a stumbling block to those around me.

When my foes seek my life, by the power of Holy Ghost, they have to flee.

So official, it's official I sit in this office.

Let every voice be silenced that speaks against it.

Anointed to cut cords and liberate God's people.

I'm not even done with 1st chapter and I'm already working on my sequel.

Deutros. The duo.

Kingdom marriages are on the horizon.

Power couples walkthrough.

Come through Divine connections.

Blessings on blessings, on blessings on top of blessings and yes there will be judgment and justice.

It is so.

Pilgrim. I'm just passing through this place.

Kairos. Now's the time. New space.

You already have the power.

So, make your next move your best move.

No longer walking in shame.

Holy Ghost in me shatters defeat,

annihilating selfish ambition and pulling down strongholds.

Jesus, the Lover of my soul.

My Maker, Creator, He is my Husband.

So, when they ask why I don't give in,

I tell them, "Because I am no longer a slave to sin."

PRETTY IN PINK

Pretty in pink, I promise to remain when my poems start to prosper.

Poised in my pink dress dressed like I'm about to receive an Oscar.

So hot check my temperature take me to the doctor Rapha.

Sophisticatingly inundating you with my lines proper,

Line upon line, line upon line, it's got to be. Truth

is they hated me for speaking the truth but they didn't understand it, and most didn't want to even stop and comprehend it. But it's OK, I'll stay

Pretty in my pink dress, as I write my lines on This pink parchment all dressed up proper.

Poised in my pink dress like I'm going to the Oscars

Do you see theses earrings have you seen these shoes?

Straight off the clearance rack

it's last season's finest.

No longer trying to save face instead I am,

pressing towards the mark for the prize of the high

calling.   Poised in my pink dress like I'm about to

receive an Oscar.

And don't worry about me trying to steal your fame,

wealth is what I'm after.

This marks the beginning of a brand-new chapter,

So once again,

just call me Ken

GIFT

So, you read my poetry thinking that I'm about you.

Truth is if I'm talking about you that I'm talking about me too,

because we have all been through something,

and sometimes we all think that what we've gone through is nothing.

But is that something that somebody else can learn from.

Our past mistakes

If we talk about our heartbreaks maybe we can take the next persons pain away,

or at least soothe it.

You know help our fellow man feel better,

when we speak the truth, we heal better,

when we communicate effectively, we can deal better,

and when we show love that's a real love letter.

We are Epistles can you read me?

I open my mouth and speak this poetry

I'm trying to get fed and then I'll feed you

I put my life on these pink pages written on cellophane paper

see-through and read through the lines as I speak to you.

I had to go deeper because I was tired of being lonely,

though I wasn't alone, I'm never alone, I was lonely.

Only. Me in my one-bedroom apartment

I cooked my meals in the microwave, and I slept on the carpet,

with my duffel bag as my pillow, and a piece of 2-yard fabric that I got from the store and a $2 throw.

me and the floor I still had to flow,

My new beginning was humble, but I wasn't humble, I was low.

Trying to come up constantly searching for mo.

My M.O. was to be a better version of me.

so I write this poetry

on the cellophane pages of my soul do you copy?

I'm an epistle, kept for the Master's use,

He uses it all, the clubs, the drugs, my bad habits

and the abuse,

He leaves nothing on the to waste

I am a gift and so are you

I am a gift; I shrink-wrapped myself and He delivered me to you.

Look at my polka dot bow, pink and brown

no clown just Ken,

I'll say it again, just in case you weren't listening,

I am a gift I wrapped myself in shrink-wrap

and He delivered me to you

if I am a gift then guess what you are too.

I KNOW WHAT YOU'RE THINKING

First, they said that I was like Jonah

and they called me a fugitive

Now they tell that they love me.

I'm not used to this madness that y'all are trying to sell

me.

Instead of putting up with this charades why don't you

just tell me.

The truth, but I guess that you're afraid

that your truth will ruin me

But it won't.

Because I already know what you're thinking.

I know the truth that's embedded in your soul

Your actions tell me so.

Your words tell me more

and even still what you don't say fills in the blanks.

So, when I speak my poetry I don't shoot blanks.

It's amazing. I mean I used to be Amazing.

He said put star at the end of your name for the wow factor, baby you'll be a star because that's what you are.

Amazing Star.

So I already know what you're thinking.

I know the words written on your soul, your actions tell me so and your words tell me more.

And whatever you don't say just fills in the blanks.

You don't even realize that God has you on a heart monitor and I'm looking through the eyes of My Father In Heaven, please forgive me.

Because when I wrote this one. I was angry.

Because they try to play me.

Like I didn't know.

And with stroke of my pen

like Moses I'm screaming out. 'let God's people Go!'

We need a deliverer, we need some deliverance.

He raised up a deliverer to come deliver us

No Bubba Sparxxx, but like Bubba Sparkxxx,

Deliverance

is on the way and it's happening now.

I was angry when I wrote this

and I tried not to sin.

To our captors let God's people go!

And from now on just call me Ken.

You act like you forgot my name but I know you didn't.

I'm the one you said would never make a million.

Look at me now I'm eating

Bank account on swole but it ain't for me it's for my people.

This ain't the sequel but it could be.

I just might make it b that way.

So don't tiptoe through the tulips on my watch.

I watch how you tried to literally kill me.

And you said that you made me.

Go ahead make me again.

But you can't can you?

Because you don't have the anecdote

Now. Let God's people Go!

This page is intentionally left blank.

Kenyetta is an Auntie, Author, occasional Personal Chef Minister, owner of Kenyetta Freeman Ventures, LLC, Dabino Publishing and prayercultureshop.com. Kenyetta enjoys reading a good book, studying the Bible and enjoying a great meal. Join the email list to stay the know. thepinkparchment.com

More by Kenyetta Freeman

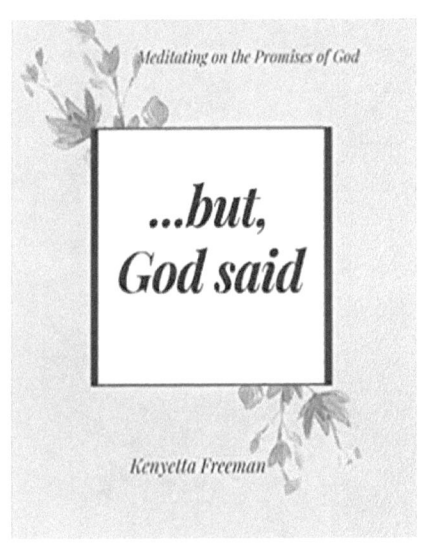

An interactive Prayer Journal with scripture art, daily confessions and prophetic poetry from the Father's heart to you.

Available on Amazon in print or digital format.

ISBN-10: 1693935775
ASIN: B07XXQ95C3

www.ingramcontent.com/pod-product-compliance
Lightning Source LLC
Chambersburg PA
CBHW050319200626
46808CB00023BA/3056